A Mustache Baby Christmas

BRIDGET HEOS *Illustrations by* **JOY ANG**

CLARION BOOKS | Houghton Mifflin Harcourt | Boston New York

Clarion Books
3 Park Avenue
New York, New York 10016

Clarion Books is an imprint of Houghton Mifflin Harcourt Publishing Company.

HMHBOOKS.COM

The text was set in Tweed SG.
The illustrations in this book were executed digitally.

Library of Congress Cataloging-in-Publication Data
Names: Heos, Bridget, author. | Ang, Joy, illustrator.
Title: A Mustache Baby Christmas / Bridget Heos ; illustrations by Joy Ang.
Description: Boston ; New York : Clarion Books, Houghton Mifflin Harcourt, [2019]
Summary: Mustache Baby wants to be a Santa's helper like Beard Baby, but after making
 a workshop full of toys he decides to keep them for himself and lands on the naughty list.
Identifiers: LCCN 2018051994 | ISBN 9781328506535 (hardcover picture book)
Subjects: | CYAC: Babies—Fiction. | Behavior—Fiction. | Christmas—Fiction. | Santa Claus—Fiction.
Mustaches—Fiction. | Humorous stories. | Classification: LCC PZ7.H4118 Mv 2019
DDC [E]—dc23 LC record available at https://lccn.loc.gov/2018051994

Manufactured in China
SCP 10 9 8 7 6 5 4 3 2 1
4500760862

For Johnny, Richie, J.J., and Sami Jeanne
—B.H.

To my aunt Joyce
—J.A.

You know that Baby Billy was born with a mustache. And that Baby Javier was born with a beard. But did you know that on Christmas Eve, Javier's beard . . .

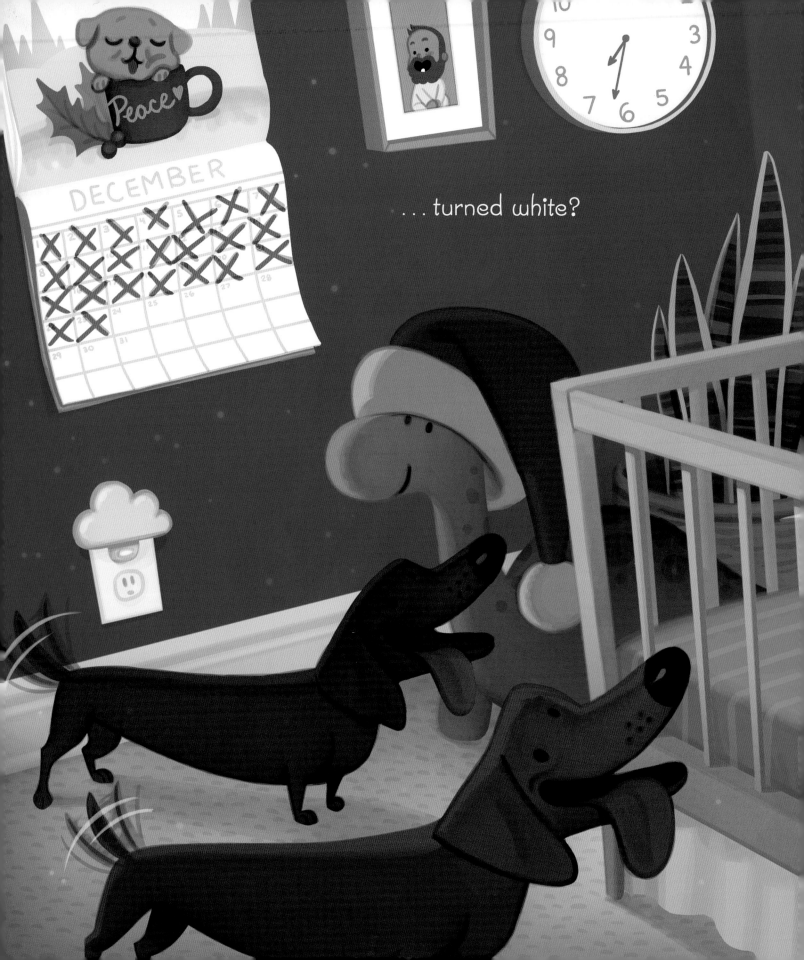

...turned white?

That made him Santa's #1 helper,
Santa Baby!

His job was to deliver presents to all the babies
in the world. There was no time to waste!

First, he listened to the babies' Christmas wishes.

Then he made a list
and checked it twice.

The babies were
mostly nice, but a few
were awfully close to
going on the naughty list!

Next, Santa Baby
readied the reindeer
for their big night . . .

... and tasted the treats that Mrs. Claus was making. (It was his duty to test each and every one.)

With the hustle and bustle of Christmas Eve,
Santa Baby hadn't had time to make the toys.

And there were
so many on the list!

Just then, Baby Billy came 'stache-ing through the snow! In a twinkling, he offered to be an elf in Santa Baby's workshop.

He toiled and tinkered in the workshop all day.

Finally, he stepped back to admire his work.

WHAT A WONDERFUL SIGHT!

So wonderful, in fact, that Billy decided to keep all the toys for himself. He had made them, after all.

Mine!

Mine!

Mine!

As the trucks, trains, and trinkets piled higher, Elf Baby's
mustache grew and curled up at the ends until he had a—

BAD GUY
MUSTACHE!

When Santa Baby came to load his sleigh, he couldn't believe his eyes! Elves were supposed to make toys, not take toys. Yet Billy had turned the winter wonderland into a winter plunder-land.

Santa Baby picked up
his crayon and scribbled
Billy's name onto
the naughty list.

That really frosted Billy's cookies! In a fit of holiday rage, he undecked the halls and snatched Santa Baby's Christmas sweets for himself.

HO HO HO
no he didn't!

Santa Baby's beard grew fluffier and fluffier until he had—
well, not a bad guy beard, because he was Santa Baby after
all, but a—

MAD GUY BEARD!

He saddled up the reindeer

and gave chase.

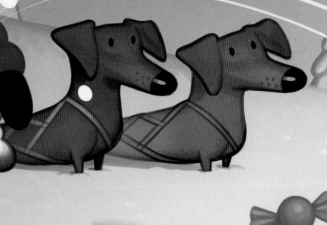

Whish whish **whish!**

Santa Baby's aim was ice-cold!

Billy dropped the treats and took cover.
Then: Ready . . .

set ...

Oh no!
Santa Baby and Elf Baby rushed
to the reindeer's aid.

They brushed the snow off him, took
him inside, and gave him a special remedy.

Billy apologized for causing all the trouble.
Filled with Christmas spirit, Santa Baby made
Billy his elf again.

Billy soon realized that it was better
to give than to receive.

Just then . . .

... jingle bells rang out overhead.
It was Santa Grownup, there to
deliver two very special presents!

First, he checked his list.

He checked it twice.

Billy had made it onto
the nice list by a hair!

Billy and Javier had done such a good job with their friends that Santa asked them to help deliver presents all over the world! Into the sleigh they hopped and off they flew.

And kids heard them exclaim, as they rode out of sight,

Merry mustache to all . . .

... and to all a beard white!